The ANIMAL TRAIN

Christopher Wormell

RED FOX

Once there was a little train that ran along a line between the driver's cottage and the town, and back again. Some days were busy and some days were not, you never could tell.

But one day the driver thought, I have a funny feeling today will be a busy one.

....And it was.

Puff-puff, chuga-chuga, puff-puff, chuga-chuga.

At Seaside Station Mrs Walrus was waiting with her shopping bag. "Lovely day for a trip into town," she said as she climbed into the pink carriage.

Oh dear, thought the driver, she's very large. She won't fit.

....But she did.

Puff-puff, chuga-chuga, puff-puff, chuga-chuga.

Down the line at Forest Station Mr Bear was waiting with *his* shopping bag. "Morning driver, morning Mrs Walrus," he said as he climbed into the yellow carriage.

Gracious me! thought the driver, what an enormous bear, he surely won't fit.

....But he did.

Puff-puff, chuga-chuga, puff-puff, chuga-chuga.

At the third station which was Jungle, Mrs Elephant was waiting with her shopping bag. Mrs Elephant simply climbed into the blue carriage.

Help! thought the driver, she'll never squeeze in.

....But she did.

Pufff-pufff, ch..chuga-chuga, pufff-pufff, ch..chuga-chuga.

My poor little train, thought the driver, it will never pull such a heavy load.
But it did.

And presently they arrived at Town Station where the three animals got out and set off for the shops.

"Don't buy too much," called the driver, a little worried. "We don't want to overload the train."

But, of course, they did. Mrs Walrus went to the fishmonger's and bought six hundred sardines.

Mr Bear went to the baker's and bought five white loaves, five brown loaves and five long French loaves, then he went to the grocer's next door and bought six large pots of honey.

Mrs Elephant went to the greengrocer's and bought apples, oranges, bananas, pears, plums, peaches, strawberries, gooseberries, mulberries, melons, mangoes, quinces, dates and a large pumpkin.

Back at the station the driver was dismayed. "Oh no!" he cried. "There's far too much, all that fruit and bread and honey, not to mention the fish. It will never fit in!"

....But it did.

Puff-puff, chuga-chuga, puff-puff, chuga-chuga.

"Not so much after all," said Mrs Walrus as the little train set off.

"Easily done," said Mr Bear.

"All a question of balance," added Mrs Elephant.
Maybe it was balance and all would have been well but at that moment a bee crawled up Mrs Elephant's trunk.
If only she had not sneezed.

....But she did.

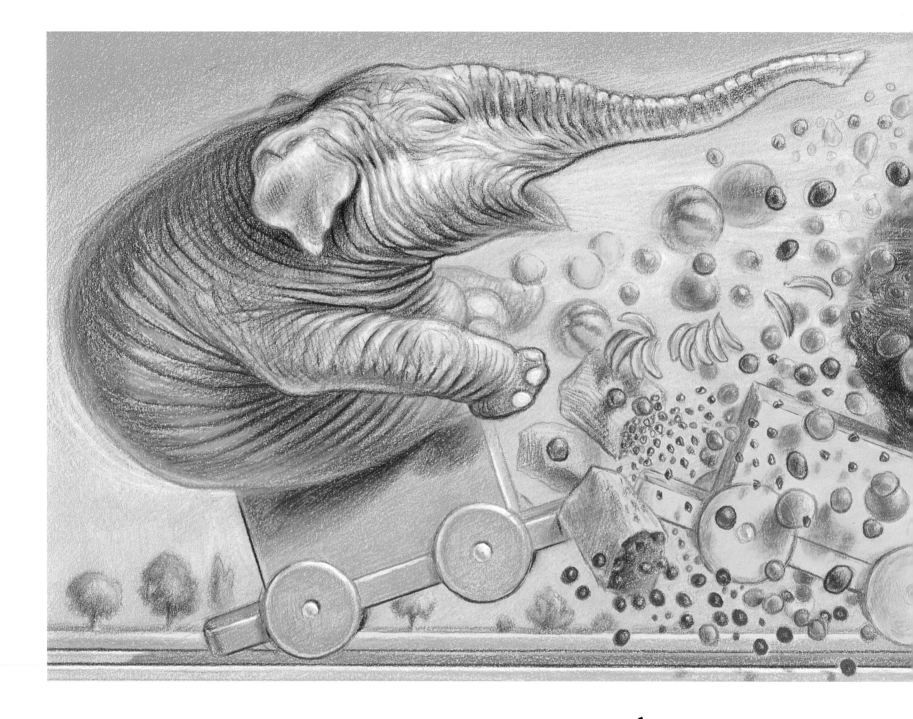

What a sneeze!

What a disaster!

"I told you so," shouted the angry driver, clutching his head. "What are we to do now?"

The animals looked round at all the food.

"Why not have a picnic?" said Mrs Elephant.

"Excellent idea," said Mr Bear.

"We can't eat all this, we need someone to share it," said Mrs Walrus.

"We'll have to call the others," said Mrs Elephant.

....So they did.

Mrs Elephant lifted her trunk and trumpeted while Mr Bear whistled and Mrs Walrus clapped her flippers and bellowed.

What a racket!

After a while they stopped and listened and faint and far off they heard a rumble which might have been the sound of heavy animals on the move.

....It was.

P resently a whole crowd of walruses and bears and elephants arrived at the side of the track.

"Anyone for a picnic?" invited Mrs Elephant.

"Sardines all round," said Mrs Walrus.

"Tuck in everybody," said Mr Bear.

....And they did.

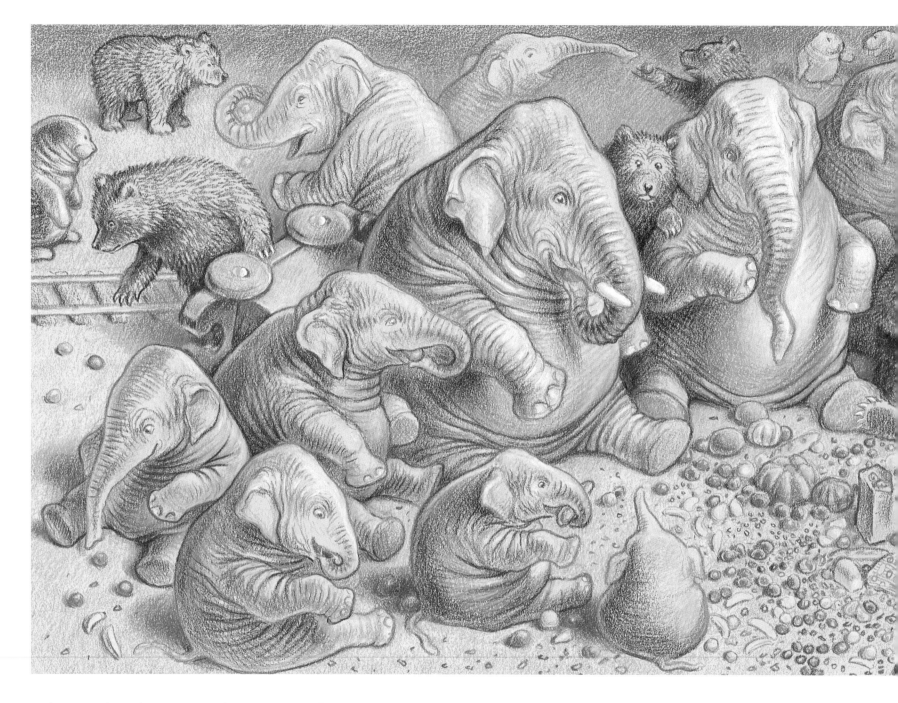

There had never been such a picnic.

There was plenty for everyone. The little elephants discovered banana sandwiches and the baby walruses tried bread and honey to see if they liked it. They did.

The little bears tried sardines and they didn't.
Only the driver was unhappy.

"What about my train?" he cried.

"No problem," said Mrs Walrus lifting up the pink carriage with Mr Walrus and the little ones lending a hand.

"Easily sorted out," said Mr Bear. He and Mrs Bear and the cubs heaved up the yellow carriage.

"All a question of leverage," said Mrs Elephant picking up the blue carriage with other elephants lending a trunk." We'll have the train set to rights in no time at all."

....And they did.

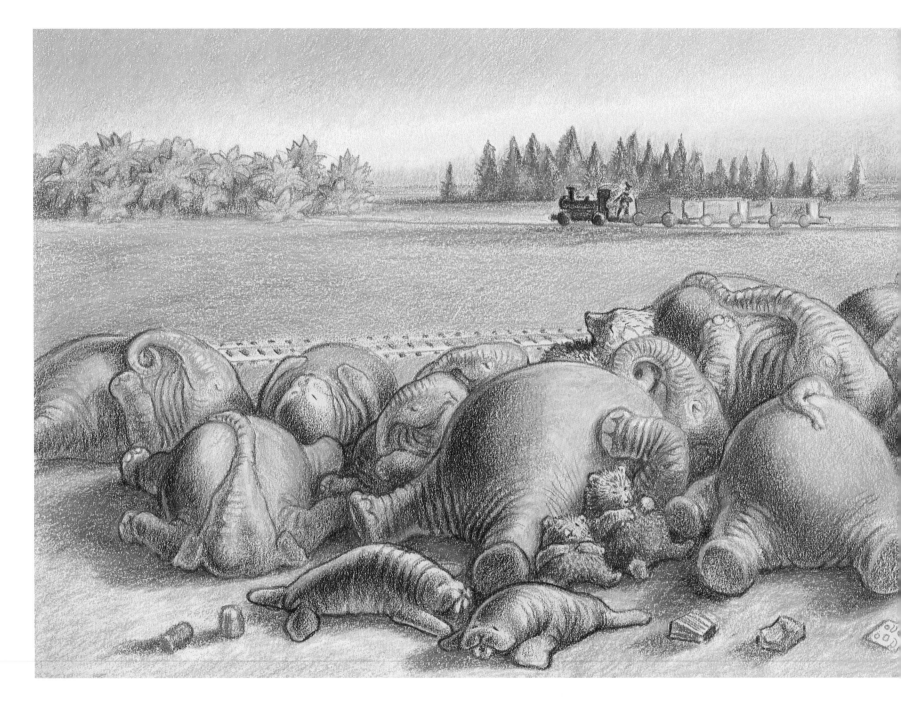

The driver was still not happy. He had a nasty feeling that all the animals might want a ride home.

But they didn't. They were all far too full and they dropped off to sleep right where they were standing.

So as the sun sank over the sea the little train wound its way homewards quite empty.
Puff-puff, chuga-chuga, puff-puff, chuga-chuga.

What a busy day, I shall sleep well tonight, thought the driver.

....And he did.

For Grandma May and Grandpa Jack

THE ANIMAL TRAIN
A RED FOX BOOK : 0 09 943306 0

First published in Great Britain by Jonathon Cape 2000
Red Fox edition published 2002

5 7 9 10 8 6 4

Red Fox Books are published by Random House Children's Books,
61-63 Uxbridge Road, London W5 5SA,
a division of The Random House Group Ltd,
in Australia by Random House Australia (Pty) Ltd,
20 Alfred Street, Milsons Point, Sydney, NSW 2061, Australia
in New Zealand by Random House New Zealand Ltd,
18 Poland Road, Glenfield, Auckland 10, New Zealand
and in South Africa by Random House (Pty) Ltd,
Endulini, 5A Jubilee Road, Parktown 2193, South Africa

THE RANDOM HOUSE GROUP Limited Reg No. 954009
www.**kids**at**random**house.co.uk

A CIP catalogue record for this book is available from the British Library.

Printed in Hong Kong